Zed Storm has lived in Japan for the past five years and is a master of several martial arts. He has a wolfhound called Max, and in his spare time plays the guitar and competes in triathlons. He likes to read about history, space exploration and rare animals and he came up with the idea for Will Solvit while camping in a Siberia

D1639008

013771633 X

www.

ATTENTION: ALL READERS!

Wherever you see something that looks like this, reach for your decoder! Holding it at the top, place the centre of your decoder over the lines. Rotate it very slowly, look closely and a picture will appear.

Mystery solved!

AND THE BATTLE OF THE NINJAS

Bath · New York · Singapore · Hong Kong · Cologne · Delhi · Melbourne

Written by Zed Storm
Creative concept and words by E. Hawken
Words by Rachel Elliot
Check out the website at www.will-solvit.com

First edition published by Parragon in 2010

Parragon
Queen Street House
4 Queen Street
Bath BA1 1HE, UK

ISBN 978-1-4454-0463-9

Printed in China.

Please retain this information for future reference.

CONTENTS

whooosh!!

?
?
?

CHAPTER ONE
MARTIAL ARTS AND MYSTERIES

You know something? Girls are M.A.D!

I'd just been swimming at the leisure centre pool and I was waiting for Zoe (my best friend) to finish her karate class. Legs and arms were flying around so fast they were just blurs! Both the girls and the boys in the class were all letting out loud yells, leaping around barefoot and throwing each other onto the padded mats.

It looked like mega-fun!

"You OK?" Zoe asked, bounding over to me while the class took a break.

"Yeah, this is kind of cool," I said.

"Cool?" Zoe exclaimed with a smirk. "What

Hi . . . YAAA!

7

happened to 'But what if a letter turns up while I'm gone?' and 'Karate's boring'?"

"Maybe I was a bit . . . hasty," I said, grinning back at her. "Seriously, Zoe, you look awesome – I had no idea you were that good!"

It was true – I was really enjoying watching her class.

"You want to join in?" she asked.

"Err…" I stuttered, not wanting to get my face smashed in by a girl. "I'm happy just watching, thanks. Plus . . . I thought it might help with my next Adventure."

I should probably explain that I'm an Adventurer, and my special skill is time travel. You think that sounds weird? Welcome to my life! It all started when I lost my parents in the middle of a prehistoric jungle, but that's a whole other story.

That would be sooo embarrassing!!

Ever since my parents went missing, I've been getting mysterious letters that appear in all sorts of crazy places. I have no idea who they're from, but I reckon the letter writer must be on my side. Without them, I'd have no idea what was going on in my Adventures. Actually, I didn't have much idea what was going on anyway, but the letters definitely helped!

"Why should coming to watch my karate class help with your next Adventure?" asked Zoe, looking confused.

"I received another letter when I got back from the future – my last Adventure," I whispered. "It said that the next one would be in the ancient past and that I'd meet Japanese ninjas!"

Before Zoe could do anything but gasp, her teacher, who they called 'Sensei', asked everyone to come and sit down in front of him.

"OK, listen up," said the teacher. "We've got a few newcomers here today, and there are some things you should know. To become truly great at karate, you need to understand a bit about its background. So this is the boring bit where you have to sit and inwardly digest."

He grinned at the class, who groaned and then laughed. He was way cooler than any of our teachers at school!

"Karate started out as a common fighting method called 'te'. It began on an island called Okinawa, was developed through sharing cultural knowledge with Chinese visitors and resulted in a ban on weapons after an invasion."

Zoe's hand shot into the air. I might have guessed – she's always the first to ask questions at school too!

"Sensei, what does karate mean?"

"Good question, Zoe," said her teacher. "'Karate' means 'empty hand', because it's a way of fighting without using weapons."

"Is it easy to learn?" asked a skinny new boy at the back.

I thought that the teacher would get cross. (My teacher, Mrs Jones, would have gone purple in the face if I'd asked her a question like that about maths!) But Zoe's Sensei just gave a little smile. He reminded me a bit of some of the great warriors I'd met in the past – he had the same quiet sense of power.

"There is no easy way to learn true karate," he said. "It's a quest for knowledge that will take a lifetime. But it's worth it! Karate can give you great skills in the fighting arts, but it can also teach you self-confidence, self-discipline, respect,

Grrrrrr!

courtesy, time management and leadership."

"How long did it take you to learn?" asked another boy.

"I am still learning," said the teacher. "For me, karate is a philosophical practice. It shows me a better way of living." He glanced at his watch and added, "And right now, that wisdom shows me that it's the end of the class! See you next week!"

Zoe waved at me as she went to get changed.

"See you outside!" she called.

I nodded and headed for the boys' changing room, where I'd left my things after swimming. I tugged open my locker and my jaw nearly hit the floor. There was a white envelope sitting on top of my damp swimming trunks, and it had my name written on it! I was shaking with excitement as I ripped the envelope open and read the letter inside.

WHAT DOES A MARTIAL ARTS' FAN EAT?
KUNG FOOD!

WILL, IF YOU THINK GIRL KARATE EXPERTS ARE
SCARY, WAIT TILL YOU HEAD OUT ON YOUR NEXT
ADVENTURE!

YOU'RE GOING TO BE VISITING FEUDAL JAPAN
AT THE TIME OF THE SAMURAI, AND THAT'S NOT
EXACTLY EVERYONE'S TOP HOLIDAY DESTINATION . . .

DON'T GO ANYWHERE WITHOUT ZOE THIS TIME -
YOU'RE GOING TO NEED HER!

I grabbed my wet swimming trunks and towel, shoved them in my backpack and then ran outside to show Zoe the letter. Typical – she wasn't there yet!

I hung around outside the girls' changing room for what felt like about ten years. Seriously, I swear it would have been quicker to run home, jump into Morph and time travel into a future where Zoe was already ready. (Morph's my dad's amazing invention – a machine that can become anything you want it to be!) I had read the leaflet on gym membership about fifteen times before she finally came out of the changing room.

"Hi, remember me?" I asked, holding out my hand. "Will Solvit, pleased to meet you."

"You're so funny I think my sides have just split," said Zoe, with a straight face. "What's the hurry, Time Boy?"

"This," I said, showing her my other hand, which contained the envelope.

Zoe gave a squeal of excitement, grabbed the letter and read it as fast as she could. Then she gave a little smile.

"What?" I asked.

"That's so sweet that you're scared of me," she said.

I nearly choked!

"I am not scared of you!" I exclaimed.

"Don't worry, I promise not to use any karate moves on you," she went on.

She was wearing a wide grin now.

"Very funny," I said, taking the letter from her. "What do you think it means?"

"For a start, I think it means that you need my super-speedy internet connection ability," she said, pulling her SurfM8 out of her pocket and

In her dreams!

hooking up to the web.

Zoe's dad works out in Singapore, and he's always sending her the latest gadgets. Some of them are mega-cool and some of them are a bit pointless, but the internet phone is easily the most useful!

"OK," she said, handing me the phone. "I've found a few pages about ninjas and samurai and stuff – check it out."

I read through the pages she had bookmarked as quickly as I could. It's amazing how much more interesting history is when you're about to become a part of it! I found out that:

- **Samurai and ninjas were both around at the same time in ancient feudal Japan.**
- **Samurai were military nobility – a mega-respected warrior class.**

- Ninjas were mostly recruited from the lower classes.
- Samurai had strict rules about honour and combat.
- Ninjas were super-secretive assassins. They would disguise themselves, spy and sabotage the enemy to complete their missions.
- Samurai were protectors of truth.
- Ninjas were mysterious and ruled by the forces of evil.

Good guys!

Bad guys!

I closed the SurfM8 and handed it back to Zoe. Her eyes were shining with excitement.

"This Adventure is going to be so cool!" she grinned.

CHAPTER TWO
WEAPON OF THE SAMURAI

The first thing we had to do before going on an Adventure was to get the grown-ups off our backs. Zoe phoned her mum to ask if she could come to Solvit Hall with me after karate class.

"Will needs some serious help with his maths project," she said into her phone as we walked home. "You wouldn't believe that someone in Year Six still uses his fingers and toes to do adding, would you?"

"Zoe!" I exclaimed.

"Thanks, Mum, see you later!" she said quickly, ending the call.

"Your mum must think I'm a total idiot," I

Well whiffy!

complained as she put her phone away.

"Well, you are a total idiot!" said Zoe.

"Takes one to know one," I said with a grin. "Come on, last one to the hall's a slug with bad breath!"

Two minutes later we were sprinting up the drive to Solvit Hall, past all the looming statues of my ancestors.

I'd lived there ever since Mum and Dad disappeared. It's Grandpa Monty's home right now, but it's been in the family for generations. Grandpa Monty shares it with his chauffeur Stanley, his dog Plato – and me.

I could hear Zoe's feet pounding on the gravel right behind me! I drew on every last bit of strength I had and hurtled towards the large wooden front door, the blood powering through my body. I was planning to use the door to stop myself but, at the last second, someone flung it wide open! I tripped over the door step and slid across the polished hall floor on my stomach like a human curling stone. Then I slammed into the panelled wall with a dull crunch.

"I won," I groaned.

Zoe was leaning against the doorframe and wheezing like an old man. Grandpa Monty, who

yum!

had opened the door, stared at me and dunked a biscuit into a cup of tea.

"You certainly know how to make an entrance, Christopher."

"My name's Will, Grandpa," I said, dragging myself to my feet and rubbing my shoulder. "Ow!"

"Any broken bones?" he enquired.

"No," I said.

"Excellent, then you can take Plato for a walk. Off you go."

"Couldn't we grab a glass of water first?" Zoe wheezed.

"Nonsense, Josephine!" said Grandpa, waving his soggy biscuit at her. "Young things like you should be out in the fresh air, not trying to demolish my oak panelling. Scoot!"

We dumped our backpacks in the hall, called

Plato and headed out into the garden.

The garden at Solvit Hall was massive! I had only just started to find my way around and I had a sneaky suspicion that there were still parts of it I hadn't yet discovered. Loads of different pathways led off in various directions and disappeared into copses or clumps of thick bushes.

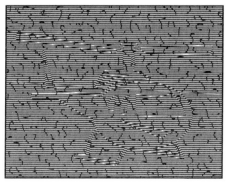

We followed the brick path around the back of the hall and past the tennis courts, towards the helicopter-landing pad.

"What do you think it'll be like?" Zoe asked, when she had finally got her breath back.

"What will what be like?" I asked.

Soooo annoying!

I was kind of distracted by Plato, who kept bringing me stuff to throw for him.

"Ancient Japan, of course," said Zoe.

I threw a deflated football that Plato had dug up from somewhere, and shrugged.

"It sounds pretty cool," I said. "All those warriors! I can't wait to meet the samurai."

"It's the ninjas I'm worried about," said Zoe. "Sensei always says that they were these super-skilful killers. What if they attack us?"

Plato ran up to me carrying a wet, muddy sock in his mouth. I think it was one of Grandpa Monty's. I picked it up between my finger and thumb and hurled it into the bushes. Plato scampered after it.

"We'll be fine," I told Zoe. "You're a match for any ninja that comes our way."

"That would be way more comforting if

→ TOTALLY gross!

24

I thought you actually knew anything about karate," my best friend replied with a laugh.

Plato emerged from the bushes dragging something furry and limp.

"Ugh, I think he's found a dead squirrel," Zoe groaned. "Gross."

"Awesome," I said.

"Will, that's disgusting!" Zoe added, turning to me in horror.

"No, not the dead squirrel," I replied. "That!"

Another white envelope was tucked into the bush behind Plato! We ran over and I tore it open.

HOW MANY NINJAS DOES IT TAKE TO SCREW IN A LIGHT BULB?
NO ONE WILL EVER KNOW - NINJAS WORK IN THE DARK!

*THERE'S SOMETHING ELSE YOU'RE GOING
TO NEED ON YOUR TRIP:*

*I'M CURVED AND YET SLENDER
AND BORN INSIDE FIRE.
I'M A BEAUTIFUL KILLER,
TO FIND ME, SEEK HIGHER . . .*

"Great," sighed Zoe. "Another cryptic clue. What's wrong with just writing down what we need to take? Why would that be so crazy?"

"Where's the fun in that?" I asked her as Plato dragged his latest find over to me. "Plato, I'm not chucking dead squirrels around the garden for you – I don't care how good you think they smell."

Pongy!

Grandpa's dog gave me a wounded look and then darted into the bushes again.

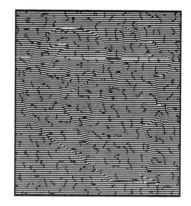

"This clue reminds me of something," I said.

"The only thing it reminds me of is how my head hurts every time we have to solve another clue," Zoe remarked. "And this one makes no sense. What's born inside fire?"

"That's it!" I yelled. "Zoe, you're a genius!"

"That's what I keep telling you, but —"

"Think about it!" I said, interrupting her. "Remember when I had that Adventure in ancient Rome and I had to take my ancestor's sword with me?"

"Yeah, but how is that –"

"It's another sword!" I exclaimed. "There are loads of them on the wall next to Titus Solvit's one. I bet there's one with a thin, curved blade."

"I get it!" cried Zoe in excitement. "The swords are kept in the attic, that's why it says 'seek higher'!"

"Come on, Plato!" I yelled. "Walkies is over – we're heading for the attic!"

Five minutes later, Zoe and I were gazing up at the sword display on the attic wall. For once I wasn't distracted by all the forgotten treasures that were hidden under the attic dust. My eyes were riveted to the curving blade of the first sword. Last time I'd looked here, I had wiped the dust off the label so that I could read it. The label said 'Samurai sword, Japan', fourteenth century.

I lifted the sword down from the wall. It had a long grip so I could hold it with both hands, and it felt good – almost as if I was holding something living. I turned it so that I could see the blade. It looked deadly sharp and it was so polished that it was as reflective as a mirror.

"Where's it from?" asked Zoe in a hushed voice.

"No idea," I said. "Let's go and ask Grandpa."

Grandpa was reading a book in the library when we went downstairs. I peered at the cover. It was called Wacky World Recipes. I showed him the sword but he shook his head.

"Never seen it before, Henry," he said. "Have you ever tried slug jelly?"

"My name's Will, Grandpa," I said, ignoring the

slug question. "How did it end up in the attic if you've never seen it?"

"There are hundreds of things in that attic that I've never seen before!" Grandpa exclaimed. "Good heavens, have you forgotten that you come from a long line of Adventurers?"

"But that's just it, Grandpa," I exclaimed. "I'm going to ancient Japan in a minute and I'm taking this sword with me. I just thought it might be a good idea to find out who it belonged to, just in case it might help me in my Adventure."

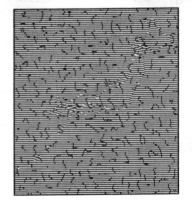

"Ancient Japan, eh?" said Grandpa. "Well well, I seem to remember something about that. You'd better have a look through my diary. See if you can find anything to help you."

When he had worked as a spy, Grandpa had kept a diary. I found it not long after moving in to Solvit Hall and it had helped me out loads of times.

"Brilliant idea, Grandpa!" I said.

Zoe and I ran back up the spiral staircase and burst into my room. I pulled the leather-bound diary out of my Adventuring backpack and started to flick through the pages, looking out for any mention of Japan. Zoe read over my shoulder, her breath tickling my ear.

"There!" she squealed, jabbing at a page with her finger.

"Don't worry, I wasn't needing my eardrum," I said, rubbing my ear.

We sat down on the end of my bed and read the diary entry.

Ouch!

October 30th, 1958

This assignment is a stinker. The letter told me that it was going to be an exciting Adventure. Ha! Five days trekking up a mountain is not my idea of exciting! I've had enough of bugs dropping on me and snakes trying to climb up my legs. I want out! Who's sending me these letters anyway? And how did that last letter end up inside my sandwich box? It makes no sense.

October 31st, 1958

I take it all back! What an incredible place. I could never have guessed that my assignment would lead me to such a beautiful land. This sacred temple has lain here, undiscovered, for hundreds of years. The Samurai Order has kept its ancient secret all that time! I hope that one day, they will be rewarded for their loyalty.

Huh?!

There was a bunch of confusing squiggles and numbers underneath the entry. I had no idea what they meant. I looked into Zoe's eyes, which glittered with excitement.

"That's where we should start!" she said. "That mountain in Japan. Your grandpa's diary entry must be a clue."

"It's as good a place as any," I agreed. "But aren't you forgetting something? We have no idea where the mountain is!"

"Call yourself an Adventurer!" Zoe scoffed. "Those squiggles and numbers are co-ordinates, Will. They're just in code, that's all. I bet Morph will be able to decipher them like that."

She clicked her fingers. As if in response, the miniature model of Morph on my bedside table started glowing. Dad's machine always shrank to a model size of the last thing it was used for when it wasn't needed, but right now it looked as if Morph was ready for an Adventure! It grew into a full sized version of a time machine and we stepped inside.

Luckily, I had packed my Adventure kit as soon as I'd received the letter telling me I was going to ancient Japan. So all I had to do was sling my backpack on my shoulder and we were set to go.

"This is so cool!" said Zoe, as we prepared for Morph to whir into action. "Japanese Adventure, here we come!"

CHAPTER THREE
AKEMI

We stumbled out of Morph, fighting the usual time-travel sickness, and found ourselves on a mountain-top. Yes! Morph had solved Grandpa's code!

The time machine shrank to a miniature version and I put it safely into my backpack.

"Will, check it out!" said Zoe in a low voice.

We were standing in front of an awesome temple. It was tall and layered like a massive wedding cake, painted red and white, and ornamented with beaten gold and strange emblems. As we gawped at it, a boy came out of the temple and walked towards us.

"Why is he wearing an apron?" Zoe whispered.

The boy was wearing dark pants and a sleeveless overall. I could see that he had a kimono underneath it. A sword like mine was tucked into his belt.

"Shh!" I hissed back.

I didn't want to offend the boy before we had even met him! The boy put his palms together and gave a little bow, so we did the same.

"Greetings, strangers," he said. "My name is Akemi."

I could feel the amulet around my neck growing hot. I had found it in one of my first letters. The amulet gets warm when it starts to translate languages, helping me to communicate with the people I meet on my Adventures. Only this time it was burning hotter than ever!

"Hi Akemi," said my best friend. "I'm Zoe and this is Will."

Suddenly I understood why the amulet was so hot. It was translating for two people instead of one! I smiled at Akemi. After all my Adventures, I'd learned that it's best to start off trusting people and take it from there.

"We're visitors," I said, "and we're not exactly sure where we are. What is this place?"

"This is the Temple of the Sun," said Akemi. "Home of the Army of the Sun."

"OK," I said. "So you're a soldier?"

"Don't be daft, Will," said Zoe. "He's not much older than us!"

"This is another time and another place," I told

her quietly. "Things are different here."

"I have just become a part of the Army of the Sun," Akemi told us.

He stood up very straight, looking strong. There was a sort of readiness about him that I hadn't noticed before.

"You're a samurai?" I guessed.

He gave another little bow, as if to say yes.

"And you?" he asked. "You are also warriors?"

"Well she's a karate expert," I said with a grin.

Akemi didn't get the joke. He just stared at me.

"We of the Army of the Sun have sworn to protect the great secret," he said. "I saw you appear out of thin air in your magical box, so I know that you are powerful. But that will not stop me from fighting you, if I must."

"I was making a joke," I said.

"A bad joke," Zoe added.

Well, I thought it was funny!

38

I thought about Grandpa's diary entry. I felt sure that this must be the same temple. If Grandpa had made friends with them, I felt sure that we could too.

"Look, Akemi, we're here to help you with whatever lies ahead," I promised him. "Please trust us – we're not your enemies!"

"I can see that great forces have brought you to the mountain," said Akemi. He looked at me as if he could read my thoughts. "You have honesty in your eyes, Will. I trust you."

"Thank you," I replied. "So tell me about your life here. What does the Army of the Sun do?"

"Forgive me," the boy said, bowing again. "I am sworn to secrecy. This is my oath. If I tell the secrets of the Sun, I will vanish into nothing – POUFF! – just as you arrived out of nowhere."

I looked around. The top of the mountain was

small and I could see all edges – but I couldn't see any steps. There wasn't even a path.

"How do you get up here?" I asked. "Is there a secret passage inside the mountain or something?"

Akemi gave me a slow smile.

"I see you carry a katana," he said.

"A katana?" I repeated. "What's that?"

"The sword of the samurai," said Akemi.

He was looking at the weapon I had taken from the attic. It was sticking out of my backpack.

"Do you know how to use it?" he asked.

"Can you show me?" I was so excited, I totally forgot that he hadn't answered my first question!

Akemi was an awesome teacher. He showed us how to hold the sword and a bunch of different cutting techniques. Zoe and I picked up the moves fairly easily, but we were nowhere near

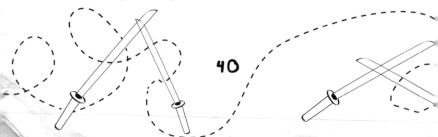

as fast as Akemi! He moved with the speed and grace of a cheetah. I bet he could have cut an opponent in two before they could blink . . . and yet he came across as so gentle!

After we had learned some of the basic moves, Akemi sheathed his sword and asked us to sit down. Suddenly I was reminded of the Sensei in Zoe's karate class.

"A calm mind is vital for the samurai warrior," said Akemi. "We use meditation to soothe our thoughts. Honour is at the heart of all we do. Poverty is no disgrace, but dishonour is like death."

His voice was soft and peaceful, and I felt myself relaxing as I listened to him.

"We follow the way of the warrior and we are loyal to our vows," Akemi went on. "Death is nothing. We do not need wealth or rich

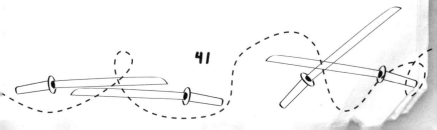

41

belongings. We believe in the seven virtues . . . rectitude, courage, benevolence, respect, honesty, honour and loyalty."

The sun was hot on our heads, but a mountain breeze cooled our skin. I closed my eyes and let Akemi's words flow over me. My thoughts drifted. I didn't know what Adventure had brought me here, and I was sure that it was something to do with the secrets of the Sun that Akemi had mentioned. But the peace of the mountain-top was getting under my skin already – I felt sure that everything would be explained sooner or later . . . when the time was right . . .

"WILL!" screamed Zoe. "RUN!"

My eyes flicked open. Arrows were flying through the air – right towards our heads!

uh-oh!

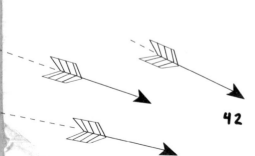

CHAPTER FOUR
THE ARMY OF THE SUN

"To the temple!" Akemi cried. "Quickly!"

As we raced towards the temple, dozens of men dressed just like Akemi came pouring out of it, their bows and arrows held ready to fire. Akemi pulled us into the temple and I raced to one of the window holes cut into the wall. I saw one of the arrows plunge through the arm of a warrior.

"Oh no!" exclaimed Zoe, who was at my side.

"It's not a fatal wound," I said, trying to make her feel better. "I saw men fight on with worse than that when I was in ancient Rome."

"I don't think he's going to be fighting on," she said.

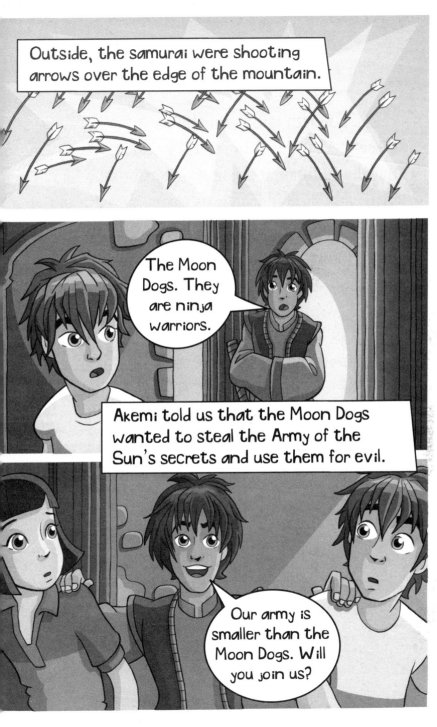

Zoe's mouth fell open, and I felt kind of like someone had just turned the world upside down. But then I thought about the warrior who had died, and the letter that had sent me here in the first place.

"I'm here on an Adventure," I said. "I reckon I need to help you guys. So I'll do whatever it takes."

Akemi beamed, but before he could say another word, I turned to Zoe.

"That doesn't apply to you," I said. 'You're not a Solvit and you're not an Adventurer. You don't have to get involved."

I saw a familiar stubborn expression cross her face. Her chin tilted higher.

"Are you crazy?" she enquired. "I might not be an Adventurer, but I'm just as brave as you are, thanks very much! There's no way I'm letting those Noon Dogs get away with this!"

"Moon Dogs," said Akemi and I together.

"Whatever."

The ninja arrows had finally stopped, and the samurai came slowly back into the temple. Six of them were carrying the fallen warrior.

"So how do we join?" I asked, trying to sound as if I wasn't thinking about poisoned arrows.

"First you must meet Shinobi," said Akemi. "He is the leader of the Army of the Sun, and the greatest living samurai. Come with me – I will take you to him."

Akemi led us deeper into the temple and stopped in front of a massive piece of silk hanging on the wall. It was very thin and fine, and it was covered with detailed painted scenes of samurai in battle.

"Wait here," said Akemi.

He stepped behind the silk hanging, and I realized that it must lead into a hidden room.

"What do you think it involves, being a samurai?" I asked Zoe in a low voice. "Apart from avoiding poisoned arrows."

"I guess . . . just being loyal and noble and stuff," Zoe whispered back. "And protecting their big secret, of course. Will, how long do you think this Adventure is going to take? Only I've got a Geography assignment due in on Monday."

"No way of knowing," I replied. "I was in ancient Rome for years, and when I came back I had hardly been gone a minute. But that visit to Egypt in 1931 lasted a day, and when I came back I'd been gone five weeks. Time travelling

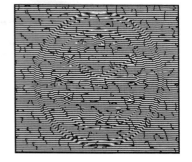

can be a bit tricky sometimes."

"Wow, that's really helpful, thanks," said Zoe, sarcastically. "I just wish we knew what you needed to do here. Do you think it's got something to do with the secret?"

"I reckon we're about to find out," I whispered, just as Akemi came back.

"Shinobi will see you now," he said.

We followed Akemi behind the silk hanging and found ourselves in a small, stark room. Pictures of samurai in battle dress were hanging on the walls. There was a thin mattress on the floor and a man was sitting cross-legged on it.

"Welcome," he said in a soft voice. "I am Shinobi."

What do you imagine the leader of a samurai army would look like? Shinobi looked nothing like how I expected! He was small, old and frail-

Wrinkly raisin face! →

looking, with a face as wrinkled as a raisin.
He must have done a ton of smiling in his life.
He had twinkling, happy eyes and a wispy
white beard.

I put my palms together and bowed. Zoe did
the same.

"I'm Will Solvit and this is my friend, Zoe," I
said. "We've come from far away to help you and
your army any way we can."

"Akemi tells me that you wish to join us," said
Shinobi.

"We'll do whatever it takes to help you stop
those ninjas," Zoe said.

"I am grateful for your friendship and your
offers of help," said Shinobi. "But not everyone is
suited to the life of the samurai."

"We're really fast learners," Zoe added.

I saw Shinobi's eyes twinkle again.

"That is good and valuable news," he said. "But not all clay can become a fine and delicate vase, and not all human beings can become samurai."

"Do you mean you don't want us?" I asked.

"You must each face a trial to find out whether you are suitable to be trained as samurai," Shinobi stated.

"What if we fail?" Zoe asked.

"Then we will still be grateful for your willingness to help, but you will be unable to do anything for us."

"What if we pass?" I asked.

That was what I was really worried about!

"Ah," said Shinobi, pressing his fingertips together and looking into my eyes. "If you pass, the secrets of the Army of the Sun will be revealed to you. And in return you must swear to protect and fight for our cause until the bitter end."

I looked at Zoe. She had gone pale.

"I meant what I said back there," I told her. "You don't have to do any of this."

"I meant what I said too," she replied. "I'm sticking by your side whether you like it or not!"

I turned back to Shinobi.

"OK, we'll do it," I said.

Shinobi looked grave and nodded.

"Then let the trials begin," he said.

Shinobi led us to a pile of three wooden planks, which were placed upon two stone blocks. Akemi stood beside his master and smiled at us in encouragement.

"I know this one!" said Zoe in excitement. "You have to chop through the wood with your bare hands."

"What?" I exclaimed.

"Zoe is correct," said Shinobi in his quiet voice.

"Don't panic," said Zoe with breezy confidence. "Sensei showed us all how to do it. I was the best in the class."

"Awesome," I said. "Then this trial is all

53

yours!"

Zoe gave a little smile and I braced myself for her screams of pain. She stepped over to the planks and planted her feet wide apart. Then she lowered her head and I heard her breathing change. It got steadier and slower. When she raised her head, her eyes were focused.

She lifted her right hand and positioned her thumb next to her forefinger, bending her other fingers a little. I watched her in fascination. She lifted her arm high up into the air, and paused. Then her hand shot downwards and went right through the wooden planks as if they were made of jelly! The six pieces clattered onto the floor.

"No – way!" I cried out in surprise.

My mouth was open so wide I felt like a goldfish.

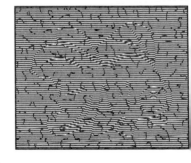

But Shinobi just gave a small smile and led us on to a table, which was covered in thin ribbons of silk.

"You have your own sword, I see," he said.

I pulled the sword out of my backpack and held it in two hands as Akemi had shown me.

"This trial will test your delicacy and control," said Shinobi. "Akemi will throw these silk ribbons into the air, and you must cut each one of them in half. If one ribbon reaches the floor intact, you will have failed."

I had no time to prepare! Akemi took a handful of the ribbons and threw them high above my head.

Focus! I thought. I knew that the worst thing I could do was to panic. I took one ribbon at a time, slicing through each piece with the sharp edge of the blade.

One – two – three – four –

I forced my breathing to stay steady . . .

five – six – seven –

I could sense Zoe's tension . . .

eight – nine – ten.

I had succeeded! But again, Shinobi said nothing. He merely raised one eyebrow.

"You know martial arts," he said to Zoe.

"Not the same ones as you . . ." she faltered.

"There are things that stay the same, wherever they have been learned," said Shinobi. "Or whenever."

For a split second his eyes met mine, and I thought I saw a wise glint in them. Then it was gone – and it had been so quick I wondered if I had imagined it.

While Akemi and I watched, Shinobi put Zoe through a series of martial-arts moves that blew my mind! Sometimes he called out words to her, and she created different positions. Then he asked her to defend herself while he attacked.

Zoe's moves were blisteringly fast, and yet I was sure that if Shinobi had chosen to, he could have broken past her defences in half a blink.

At last they stopped and bowed to each other. Shinobi's eyes turned to me again.

"The final trial is yours," he said. "Come."

When I saw what he wanted me to do, I almost wished I could just dodge a few poisoned arrows instead. A bed of burning-hot coals lay in front of me and I had to walk across them, barefoot. I felt sick and dizzy.

Then I remembered my dad talking about firewalking. He was an inventor so he was interested in the physics of things. He had once told me that the trick to firewalking was to

Hot, hot, hot!

remember that the coals had burned down to pure carbon, like charcoal. I closed my eyes and I could almost hear his excited voice.

"You see, Will, the lightweight carbon is a really bad heat conductor," he had said at the time. "It takes a while for heat to transfer from the glowing coal to your skin. By walking fast, your feet never get hot enough to burn."

I opened my eyes and nodded. I could do this!

I took off my shoes and socks, and stood at the far end of the coal bed. Zoe was waiting at the other end.

"Will . . ." she began.

But there was nothing to say. This had to be done if we were going to help the Army of the Sun. I stood up straight, breathed in, and stepped onto the coals.

I was ready for pain but instead it was just a

bit ticklish! I walked fast (without running) and, before I knew it, I was stepping off the other end.

"Will, that was amazing!" Zoe exclaimed.

"You have both done well," said Shinobi. "You have passed our tests. You will join us."

He led us through another silk tapestry. I expected to be in a small room like the one before, but this time we found ourselves in a beautiful water garden. Shinobi and Akemi stayed back as we moved further in.

I guessed that we were at the heart of the temple. In the middle of the room was a bubbling fresh spring that seemed to be rising up out of the earth. It was surrounded by a circle of golden cups.

"Awesome," I said, taking a step forwards.

On the far side of the room was a spectacular samurai sword standing on a platform. It was polished to a mirror finish like mine, but this was so shiny that it seemed to glow with its own light. The blade was engraved with what looked like Japanese symbols.

"What do they mean?" asked Zoe.

"I don't . . . wow . . ."

I felt my amulet burning against my chest again, and suddenly the weird shapes and squiggles on the sword made sense.

"They say 'Once you have drunk from the Spring of Truth then you will ride the wind forever,'" I read aloud.

"What's the Spring of Truth?" asked Zoe.

"What does 'ride the wind' mean?" I wondered.

"Come," said Akemi, beckoning Zoe and me to follow him. "Come and find out."

He led us over to the spring in the middle of the room and offered each of us one of the golden cups. They felt warm and heavy. Akemi smiled at us.

"You mean . . . you want us to drink?" asked Zoe.

Akemi just blinked and smiled again. We kneeled beside the spring and let the water bubble into the cups. Then, keeping our eyes on each other, we raised the cups to our lips.

Grandpa Monty would go officially nuts for that water! It tasted like every delicious thing you ever thought of eating or drinking, all rolled into one. I couldn't even decide if it was warm or cold. I just knew that it was the best thing I'd ever drunk. I closed my eyes and let the taste froth around my mouth.

Suddenly I noticed that my legs and feet were tingling. It was kind of like pins and needles plus that lightheaded feeling you get on a rollercoaster.

"Will!" squeaked Zoe.

I opened my eyes. She looked as if she were stuck halfway between completely terrified and totally ecstatic.

"What?" I asked.

"Look down!"

I did as she said, and my eyes did roly-polies in their sockets.

We had risen three feet off the ground!

AWESOME!

CHAPTER SIX
THE ART OF FLIGHT

Half an hour later, we were sitting cross-legged on the mountain-top, listening to Shinobi. We had made our oaths of allegiance and were now members of the Army of the Sun. Samurai warriors were all around us, soaring through the air. I was starting to get 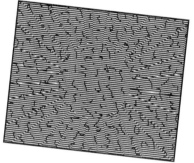 used to it now but Zoe still looked a bit shocked.

"Once, many long winters ago, the Moon Dogs and the Army of the Sun were one large band of warriors," said Shinobi. "They had all sworn to protect the Spring of Truth."

"What split them up?" I asked.

"Not all members of that ancient order were content to stay on the mountain-top," the samurai master explained. "They wanted to use the spring's power to ride the wind throughout the world. They wanted to use their power to terrify and control others, and to win in battle. But the true defenders of truth knew that this would only lead to terrible wars amongst mankind."

"Why?" asked Zoe.

"Can you imagine what would happen if the world knew about the Spring of Truth?" asked Shinobi with a sad smile.

"They would drink it dry," said Akemi. "All its gifts and wonders would be lost forever."

Shinobi nodded.

"So the ancient fellowship fought a bitter

WILL'S FACT FILE

ear Adventurer,

f you've already read about my adventures in Japan, you should know something about the samurai and their arch-enemy, the ninjas. But allow me to tell you more. The samurai and ninjas were both highly trained warriors in feudal Japan. Much has been written about the samurai because they were a major force in ancient Japan. Not quite so much is known about the ninjas, who were like very secretive secret agents.

Check out more facts and stats about these formidable warriors.

SAMURAI TIMELINE

400s AD
Horses are introduced to Japanese fighting.

500s
Buddhism arrives in Japan and quickly becomes a powerful philosophy for rulers and warriors.

900s
The samurai class gains strength in the countryside.

1192
Yorimoto becomes first permanent shogun (samurai general) of Japan, and the samurai effectively rule Japan for the next 600 years.

1274
The samurai defeat the Mongol invaders after many years of fierce fighting.

1400s
Master swordsmen establish dojo (training schools) to teach kenju (martial art using a sword).

1467–77
The Onin War sees the decline of shogun power and begins the Sengoku Jidai (The Age of the Country at War).

1603–1868
Shoguns rule feudal Japan with the samurai at the top society, followed by farmers artisans and traders.

1703–08
Earthquakes, floods and fires ravage Japan, Mount Fuji erupts and a measles epidemic breaks out.

1854
Japan starts trading with the United States

1867
Emperor Mutuhito regains his traditional powers and takes the name Meiji.

1873
Emperor Meiji establishes a conscript army, open to anyo

1876
Emperor Meiji bans the wearing of swords.

THE SAMURAI:

- were a warrior class.
- were professional soldiers.
- were skilled in martial arts.
- used various weapons including the bow and arrow and the sword.
- were also great horsemen.
- name means 'to serve'.
- followed a code of honour, called the Bushido.
- were honourable, loyal and honest.
- didn't fear death.
- would rather die than face defeat.
- included women.

THE NINJAS:

- were well-paid professionals.
- were spies, assassins and terrorists.
- were disloyal and would fight for whoever paid them the most.
- often featured in myth, with supernatural powers.
- were secretive, shadowy figures.
- were masters of disguise.
- could fade into the shadows and sneak around.
- practised ninjutsu — the art of stealth.
- are called shinobi in Japan.
- had no honour, were dirty fighters and were feared by the samurai.

Samurai society

The samurai lived in a feudal society ruled by the shogun.

- Beneath the shogun were the daimyo or local lords.
- Each daimyo had their own group of samurai.
- Ronin samurai were masterless because their master had died or they had lost favour with them.

The samurai were totally loyal to their daimyo.

The way of the warrior

Samurai led their life according to the Bushido. It said a Samurai should:

- be loyal to his or her master, even when faced with death.
- be self-disciplined and ready to fight at all times.
- be respectful of others.
- be a master of the martial arts.
- have freedom of fear, which meant they shouldn't fear death.

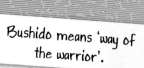

Bushido means 'way of the warrior'.

A Samurai's rights and duties

A samurai had privileges as well as obligations.

- Samurai were the only people allowed a first name and a surname.
- They were also allowed a family crest.
- They could kill any commoner offended them.

Only the samurai were allowed to carry, and use, two swords.

Samurai arms and armour

The armour and weapons a samurai wore weren't just for fighting; they were designed to look ferocious.

Their ornate helmets were called kabuto.

The box-like armour they wore for mounted battle was called the o-yoroi, or great armour.

The famous samurai sword, or katana, had a sharp, curved blade.

The mempo was a terrifying face mask.

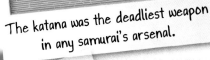

The katana was the deadliest weapon in any samurai's arsenal.

The katana

The katana, or samurai sword, was a symbol of great pride.

· It had a single edge and a long grip.
· It was handcrafted by highly respected blacksmiths.
· It was first developed in the 10th century.
· It remains an iconic symbol of Japan and its history.

Rules of engagement

The samurai were highly disciplined in everything they did — even charging into battle.

Samurai fought one-on-one.

A samurai called out his family name, rank and accomplishments as he went into battle.

He then sought out an opponent with similar rank.

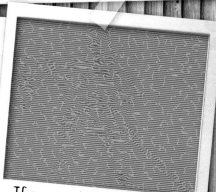

If a samurai beat his opponent, he would take his head as victory.

Samurai training

Anyone could become a samurai until the sixteenth century when you had to be from the right, aristocratic family.

- Samurai training began at the age of three.
- Later, trainees were taught military tactics and unarmed combat.
- They were also expected to be well read, poetic, thoughtful and spiritu

They were taught how to be excellent horsemen.

Genpuku

Between the ages of twelve and eighteen a trainee became a full-fledged samurai in a ritual called genpuku.

- The new recruits were given a samurai name.
- They were presented with a wakizashi, a shorter sword than the katana.
- They also wore a katana.
- They were allowed to marry.

They adopted the samurai hairstyle.

Samurai daily life

When the samurai weren't fighting they led a privileged and surprisingl respectable life.

- From the sixteenth century they lived in castle barracks.
- Samurai spent a great deal of time appreciating the arts.
- They ate with chopsticks.
- They practised Zen Buddhi

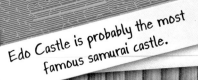

Edo Castle is probably the most famous samurai castle.

Samurai clothing and hair

The samurai took great care with their personal appearance. They bathed and shaved every day, and even manicured their nails.

· They styled their hair into a topknot, called a 'chomage'.
For battle they shaved the tops of their heads to keep cool.
They wore sword-belts called 'obi'.

When they weren't fighting, samurai wore a plain, silk komono.

Who were the ninjas?

According to Japanese mythology the first ninja descended from a demon that was half man and half crow. But, obviously, this wasn't the case.

· Ordinary ninjas were often peasants with a talent for fighting.
· Many of their skills were learnt from Chinese warrior monks.
· Samurai enemies employed them.

Some of the ninja leaders were disgraced samurai.

Female ninjas

Women who became ninjas were known as kunoichi.

· They received different training to male ninjas.
· They used their beauty and charm to get close to the enemy.
· They would conceal weapons up their sleeves or in their hair.

Some female ninjas pretended to be geisha to trick a victim.

Ninja equipment

Ninjas often wore plain clothing so that they wouldn't stand out.

· At night they sometimes wore a dark jacket, black trousers, black sandals and a loose hood.
· They often carried a ninja-to (short sword) slung across their backs.
· They fought with sharp metal fans.
· They also used farm tools, like saw and pruning shears, as weapons.

They wore shuko (brass knuckles) or vicious hand claws.

Ninja techniques

In ninjutsu just about anything went but most ninjas were highly trained fighters.

· Karate was passed on to the ninjas by the Chinese warrior monks.
· Blade throwing was an essential skill.
· They used fire and water as weapons.
· Ninjas were masters of disguise and concealment.
· Many ninjas were expert poisoners.
· Ninjas were often explosive experts.

Ninjas were deadly with just about any weapon, including throwing stars.

Supernatural ninjas

Over the centuries, people grew so scared of ninjas that tales of their supernatural powers grew. These super-ninja were said to have the power of invisibility and be:

· over 2 metres tall.
· three-headed demons.
· ghosts or spirits that could change shape.

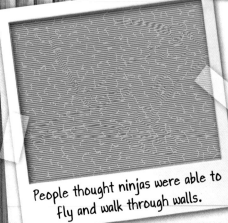

People thought ninjas were able to fly and walk through walls.

war," he went on. "The treacherous warriors lost and fled from the mountain. But they have been waiting for a time when they can attack the Army of the Sun and claim the spring for themselves. Their descendants cannot fly as we can, but their ninja abilities grow stronger, and our Army grows smaller."

I thought about the ninjas shooting their evil arrows at the flying samurai. For a moment I got that rollercoaster feeling again. The Army of the Sun could fight in mid-air and soar through the skies . . . and now, so could we.

"The time is coming when you will need to use your skills," Shinobi told us. "You must learn what you can now, before the battle begins. There is so little time."

"Let me teach them, Master," said Akemi.

Shinobi put his palms together and bowed. It

was time for us to go – and I couldn't wait to get started!

'No wonder the Moon Dogs want to get to the Spring of Truth,' I thought as I rose into the air. 'This is AWESOME!'

Akemi had led us halfway down the mountainside, until we were hovering above a canopy of trees. There was no way that the Moon Dogs would be able to see us from the ground – we were free to practise.

"The first thing to learn about 'flying martial arts' is agility," said Akemi. "It's more like being in water than like being on land. You can flip, roll and dive to avoid your opponent. Watch!"

He gave a sudden leap and flipped a

somersault in the air, then dived sideways, back-flipped and scissor-kicked above our heads.

"Wicked!" I exclaimed.

"Try it yourselves," Akemi insisted.

Zoe and I leaped into the air at the same time, bumped into each other and ended up crashing into a treetop. Akemi tried to hide a smile.

"Focus all your energies on the sensation of your body moving through the air," he said. "Become a part of the element of air. You must move as if you are flying on the breath of the world."

"The breath of the world?" Zoe repeated. "What's that?"

"The wind," said Akemi, lifting his hands as if he were calling the breeze to him. "You are riding the wind."

I thought about what he was saying, and tried

67

to get a sense of the air around me. Riding the wind felt a bit like standing on a bouncy castle (except without the stinky plastic under your feet and the four-year-old kids trying to dive-bomb each other). I sort of bounced up and down a couple of times, and then tried a somersault. It was a bit wonky and I nearly hit Akemi, but it felt a bit more controlled.

"Better," said Akemi. "Keep trying."

Zoe and I practised for about half an hour, with Akemi watching and gently encouraging us. I really started to get the feel for flying moves – it was a bit like that feeling you get when you've been totally rubbish on a computer game and then it suddenly clicks into place. One minute I was flailing around and colliding with spiky treetops, and the next minute I was completely in the zone.

"Good," said Akemi, when we were both able to complete precise somersaults and backflips. "These are the moves you will need to escape the Moon Dogs and their weapons."

"I don't get it," said Zoe, doing mid-air handsprings in slow motion. "I mean, we can fly. How can the Moon Dogs possibly defeat us?"

"Because they are master assassins," said Akemi. "Make no mistake, Zoe, you must learn how to keep yourself out of their clutches. A Moon Dog ninja can kill with one blow from a single arrow."

"You've taught us about defence, but what about attack?" I asked. "Shouldn't we be learning to battle too?"

"You have great skills, but you are not fully trained samurai," said Akemi. "It is unlikely that a ninja will give you a chance to get in a lucky blow. You will need defence skills to survive the upcoming battle . . . as will we all."

The sun was sinking behind the mountain-top when we finally headed back to the temple. Akemi had shown us so many defence moves that I felt as if he had put me in a bottle and shaken it up and down. Akemi was probably feeling a bit responsible for our safety because it was he who had first suggested that we join the army.

When my feet touched the ground, my legs wobbled and I staggered sideways. Akemi laughed and grabbed my arm.

"It is a strange feeling at first," he said, "but it gets easier."

"Look!" Zoe exclaimed, landing beside us and clutching on to me as her legs wobbled too.

She pointed at the temple entrance. Master Shinobi was standing there, and the twinkle had completely left his eyes. He looked old and sad.

We hurried towards him and bowed.

"What is wrong, Master?" Akemi asked.

"There is bad news," said Shinobi. "The Moon Dogs have been on the side of the mountain. They're on their way up."

I felt that shiver down my spine again. I hadn't set eyes on a ninja, but the thought of them made me feel cold.

"How far away are they?" asked Akemi.

"One more sunrise and they will be among us," said Shinobi. "I will guard the spring myself, but everyone else will be needed for the great battle."

Zoe's eyes met mine.

"I guess that means us," she said.

CHAPTER SEVEN
THE ENEMY CAMP

I was shattered after all the training with Akemi, but I needed to clear my head, and mid-air seemed like a pretty good place to do it. I rose into the sky, got into a sitting position and allowed the breeze to blow me gently towards a tall clump of trees on the side of the mountain.

Zoe soared up to join me.

"You OK?" she asked.

I was feeling a bit freaked-out about the battle ahead, but there was no way I was telling her that!

"Yeah, just thinking," I said.

"About . . .?"

"Well, Akemi says that we're not experienced enough to fight the Moon Dogs," I said, "and I guess he knows what he's talking about. But if we're not going to be much use in battle, what's the point of being here? I mean, what's the Adventure?"

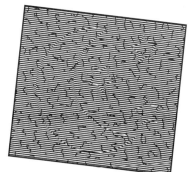

I looked at Zoe, but she suddenly looked as if she were going to explode with excitement.

"Maybe that'll have the answers," she said.

A white envelope was tucked into the top of the nearest tree! I floated towards it and ripped it open (this HAD to be one of the best ways to open a letter yet – in mid-air)!

WHAT DO YOU CALL A PIG THAT DOES KARATE?
A PORK CHOP!

YOU AND ZOE BOTH DID A GREAT JOB OF
GETTING THROUGH THE TRIALS. WELL DONE!
DON'T WORRY - EVERYTHING'S GOING EXACTLY
THE WAY IT SHOULD. BUT THERE'S NOTHING YOU
CAN DO TO HELP THE ARMY OF THE SUN IF YOU
STAY ON THE MOUNTAIN-TOP.

BRACE YOURSELF, WILL.

YOU ARE GOING TO HAVE TO SNEAK INTO THE
MOON DOGS' CAMP TONIGHT.

I flew down to the temple as fast as I could.
"Will, wait up!" Zoe called behind me. "What

are you going to do?"

"Show Shinobi the letter," I said. "We've sworn loyalty to the Army of the Sun, so that means he's in charge."

"Yeah, but if you tell him about the letter, he'll want to know who sent it and how you know you can trust them," Zoe said. "Wouldn't it be better to skip that part?"

She had a point. It's not exactly easy trying to persuade people I'm a time traveller, let alone the fact that I get mega-weird anonymous letters that help me through my Adventures!

"So you see," I was saying to Shinobi ten minutes later, "Zoe and I can't be much use in battle, but maybe we can do something else to

help. We're the smallest members of the Army of the Sun – we could sneak into the Moon Dogs' camp and try to find out about their battle strategy."

"Spying is not the samurai way," said Shinobi.

"We've made an oath," I said. "We're not going to do anything dishonourable. But this is one way that we can fight for the spring. There are so few of us. Surely the most important thing is to protect the spring?"

Shinobi closed his eyes and sat very still. A breeze ruffled his wispy white hairs.

"Your reasoning is sound," he said at last, opening his eyes. "Very well, go and see what you can discover."

Zoe and I didn't waste a second of our time. We bowed and rose into the air, then flew over the edge of the mountain and down towards the place where we knew the enemy had camped for the night.

Night had fallen and the moon was gleaming above our heads, looking like a white globe in the sky. It helped us to find the spot where the ninjas were resting, but then we had to land behind a clump of bushes. We couldn't risk one of them spotting us silhouetted against the moon!

The Moon Dogs were all dressed in black and

Knew this would come in handy!

wearing black masks. They were sitting cross-legged around a fire and talking in low voices.

I put my mouth against Zoe's ear and spoke with a lisp so that the ninjas wouldn't hear any hissing sounds. (That's a trick Mark Antony taught me back in Roman times.)

"We'll have to get clother to lithen to what they're thaying."

Zoe nodded. We both rose a few centimetres off the ground and drifted a little closer, still staying low behind the bushes. As soon as I could hear what was being said, I held up a hand to tell Zoe to stop.

"My brothers," I heard one of the ninjas say. "Dawn will bring a new era to the world. For centuries the Moon Dogs have been pushed out and ignored by the Army of the Sun. Tomorrow, all that will change!"

I guessed that he must be the leader. There was a muted mutter of approval from the other masked men around the fire.

"They will not expect an attack so soon after the skirmish yesterday," the leader went on. "They may have the advantage of flight, but we have spent centuries developing our battle techniques. At dawn, we will pull these self-righteous fools out of the sky and crush them beneath our feet!"

Zoe put her hand on my arm and whispered in my ear.

"They're attacking at dawn," she said, still lisping. "Come on, we have to warn Thinobi."

"You go," I said. "I'll wait – maybe I can find a way to hold them up."

Zoe nodded and slipped away silently. I continued listening to the ninja leader. He sounded boastful, arrogant and cruel – pretty much the exact opposite of Shinobi.

"We cannot fail now," he was saying. "This is our time, my brothers – the time of the Moon Dogs! We'll rule the world!"

"Master," said one of the men, "what if the Army of the Sun have been developing new battle techniques too?"

"Snivelling coward, are you afraid?" the leader sneered. "What is there to fear? Our techniques are unbeatable and we have our magic dragon-scale swords. Even if your fighting skills are not good enough, the magic of the dragon scales will repel any enemy."

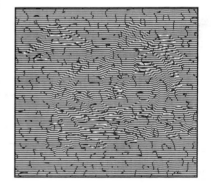

BINGO!

That was my mission! I knew it the second I had heard it. However dangerous it was, I somehow had to take those swords. If the Moon Dogs attacked with them, the Army of the Sun didn't stand a chance.

I have no idea how long I waited for the Moon Dogs to fall asleep. Hours passed and the moon rose high in the sky. I was a bit worried because it was so bright, but then I got lucky. A whole bunch of clouds rolled over and sank the mountainside into pitch darkness.

At last, all the ninjas except one were lying on their sides around the dying embers of the fire. I just had to find a way to get past the ninja on guard duty.

Suddenly I realized that I was still carrying my backpack – and my Adventure kit was inside! I took it off my back and slowly unzipped it one tiny piece at a time. I couldn't risk being heard! Finally I opened it wide enough to reach inside.

The first thing that my fingers found was my night-vision goggles. Perfect! I put them on and gazed over at the fire. Now I could clearly see the guard pacing around the circle of sleeping Moon Dogs.

I reached into my bag again and this time I felt the familiar shape of my stun gun. Yes! That was exactly what I needed. I switched on the silencer mode, aimed it at the guard and pulled the trigger.

There was a hushed POP and a flash of

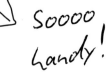
Soooo
handy!

82

blue light. The guard crumpled to the ground without a murmur. So far so good . . . now all I had to do was steal the swords. The only trouble was that all the ninjas were wearing their swords in their belts.

This was not going to be easy.

Have you ever played a game called buzz wire? There's a metal loop around a long, twisted piece of wire, and you have to move the loop from one end of the wire to the other without touching the loop to the wire. It takes a really steady hand.

Well, taking the ninjas' swords was a bit like playing a really scary game of buzz wire . . . except that if I made a mistake, I wouldn't get an electric buzzer sound – I'd get a ninja sword through my belly.

While the Moon Dogs slept, I flew from ninja to ninja, easing their swords out of their sheaths. Slowly . . . slowly . . . I drew the swords towards me, holding my breath and freezing each time I made the slightest noise. It was a good thing that they had spent the day climbing the mountain – they were all exhausted and in a deep sleep.

One after another I gathered the swords. Each time I got a new one, I flew up and hid it high above their heads, in the thick treetops. The trees grew thick with the shining curved blades, until they looked like polished branches sticking up out of the greenery.

I left the guard till last, because I knew that my stun gun had knocked him out and I wouldn't have to be so careful. That proved to be a BIG mistake! By the time I finally reached him, the effect of the stun gun had totally worn away. I pulled his sword from its sheath in one long, slow movement, but as the tip was released, I felt a strong hand close around my ankle like a band of steel.

"Thieves!" he yelled. "Attackers! Brothers, awake!"

All around me, the ninjas sprang to their feet. I was doomed.

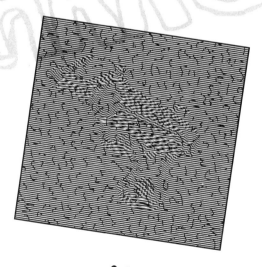

I grasped the guard's sword with both hands, preparing to fight, but suddenly his hand jerked off my ankle as if someone had pulled him away. I didn't waste my time wondering what had happened! I shot upwards towards the trees and plunged the final sword among the leaves.

Below me, I could hear the angry shouts of the ninjas as they discovered that their weapons were missing. Relief and delight rose up inside me like bubbles. I had done it! I had stopped the ninjas without the need for a battle.

I stayed hidden among the treetops, listening to their angry words.

"You were supposed to be guarding the camp, not sleeping!" I heard the leader shriek in high-pitched fury.

"There was a blue flash and something hit me, Master," said the guard.

"No excuses are acceptable. We have lost every sword in the camp! After spending decades gathering enough dragon scales to make them, they are now all gone. Years have been wasted thanks to your incompetence."

I grinned. Now they would have to turn back. But the leader's next words made me feel sick.

"Now you will have to work twice as hard to defeat the samurai," he said. "The swords would have made our task simple, but we are ninjas! We can conquer these arrogant warriors with our bare hands if we must."

Suddenly a faint light broke around me. I

pulled off my night-vision goggles and looked up. High above, I could see the edge of the mountain-top. Faint swirls of blue mist were hanging around it like curls of smoke, and the dawn light was shining through them. It looked so peaceful and magical that it was hard to believe anything violent was about to happen there.

Then I looked back down at the ninja camp and it was like being in a nightmare. The assassins were standing in neat formations, ready for the attack. Their leader was walking among them.

"This final section of the mountain is the most difficult," he was saying. "Use your throwing stars to pull yourselves up. Stay in formation and be ready for anything!"

I watched as each ninja warrior pulled out

Mega sharp!

a thin, flat plate of metal. Every plate had four sharpened points and a hole in the centre. Their leader gave the word and the assassins surged forwards to the mountainside. They jabbed their throwing stars into the rock and used them to heave themselves up. Then they pulled the stars out of the rock and repeated the same thing further up. They were using the stars like ice picks on the side of a glacier!

There was nothing more I could do here. I shot upwards with all the strength and speed I could find and burst through the blue mist to the mountain-top. It was bathed in the dawn light and the sun was glittering on the armour and weapons of every samurai warrior on the mountain. Zoe had warned them and they were ready.

I landed beside Shinobi and bowed.

"I tried to stop them," I began, sadly, guilt clutching at my insides. "I took their magical swords but it has not stopped them from attacking. They are climbing the mountain now and I don't think battle can be avoided."

Shinobi looked into my eyes.

"Guilt is not a helpful emotion to hold on to," he said. "You have done well. The Army of the Sun is preparing for battle."

He swept his hand out and I looked at the brave warriors that surrounded me. They looked mega-cool. Their armour was colourful and big and bold. They were all busy – some were still pulling on their battle robes, others

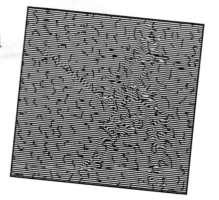

were performing sword ceremonies in small groups. Some were practising in the air above our heads, their light, panelled armour flicking out around them as they somersaulted and flipped through the sky.

"Will!" called Zoe, rushing up to me. "Where have you been?"

I explained what I had done with the swords, and she high-fived me.

"That's awesome!" she said. "I don't know how you had the nerve!"

Before I could reply, there was a shout from the warriors on guard at the mountain-top edges.

"They're coming!"

"Get ready!"

The samurai formed a solid square formation, with warriors facing all directions.

"Zoe, Will, I wish you to stay out of this

battle," Shinobi said.

"But –"

"Stay back and observe from a distance," he continued, as if I hadn't spoken. "In the heat of combat, it is not possible to see the shape of the battle. You have powers I cannot understand, and only by watching how the battle unfolds will you know how best to use them."

"Samurai, stand ready!" cried the guards.

This was not the time to argue! Zoe and I rose above the mountain-top and hovered beside the temple. There was a split second of silence. It was as if every samurai on the mountain-top was holding their breath. Then a black wave of ninjas broke over the edge and surged towards the samurai like an oil slick. The battle had begun!

It was like watching a DVD on fast forward! The samurai and the ninjas were so fast that my brain wouldn't accept it was real.

I saw Akemi flip through the air and use his feet to send a ninja flying backwards over the edge of the mountain-top.

Then I saw a ninja leap high into the air as if he were on springs and scissor-kick a samurai, who was thrown against the temple wall with a

sickening CRUNCH.

Shinobi was a streak of mercury, moving faster than the eye could see. He seemed to be everywhere at once.

The ninja leader had a spinning move that pretty much turned him into a human drill. He was using it to knock samurai out of the air, then he was finishing them off with a single chop of his hand.

"Oh wow," said Zoe, gulping. "We would so not survive out there."

I had thought that the Army of the Sun had a massive advantage because they could fly. But the ninjas were so good, the samurai had to be super-careful. The minute one of them was knocked to the ground, a bunch of ninjas would swarm all over them.

"There are so many of them!" I groaned, as

another oil slick of Moon Dogs came pouring over the edge of the mountain-top.

"If they keep going like this, they're going to beat us," said Zoe. "There are just too many of them."

I didn't reply – my eyes were glued to Akemi, who was locked in fierce combat with a ninja twice his size. He was hovering in the air just to make himself the same height as his 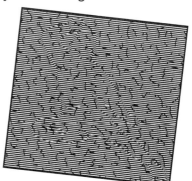 opponent, and their arms and legs were chopping and blocking so fast it made me dizzy.

Akemi grabbed the ninja's foot as it jabbed at his chest. In one single, fluid movement, he twisted the foot and pushed the ninja away.

The ninja hurtled through the air, rolling out of control. He yelled as he dropped over the edge of the mountain. I heaved a sigh of relief but it only lasted a second before Akemi was locked in combat again.

I stared around the battlefield, my throat burning with the sudden urge to be sick. Zoe was right – there were too many ninjas and not enough samurai. It was just a matter of time before the Army of the Sun was destroyed!

CHAPTER NINE
DESPERATE MEASURES

I shivered as I thought about the ninja guard who had nearly captured me. For the first time, I wondered what had made him let me go. What had I been doing? I had grabbed his sword with both hands and then, for some reason, he had pulled his hand off my ankle as if it were red-hot.

"If only we had something that would just scare them off," said Zoe.

She looked miserable and helpless. I stared at her. Then suddenly I remembered the Moon Dog leader's words. The magic of the dragon scales will repel any enemy. That must be what had happened at the camp! The guard was my enemy and the dragon-scale sword hadn't let him touch me. It obviously worked for the last person holding the sword!

"That's it!" I exclaimed, starting forwards.

Zoe grabbed my arm.

"You are not going out there to fight!" she exclaimed.

"You're right, I'm not," I said. "But I am going to get the Moon Dogs off this mountain-top – once and for all. I've had an idea!"

"Look out!" Zoe screamed.

A samurai warrior had been caught off guard and thrown towards us like a human cannonball, head first. Without thinking, I darted in between him and the temple wall.

OOOPH!

His head hit my stomach.

THUD!

My back hit the wall. All the breath was knocked out of me and I felt myself dropping towards the ground. The warrior I had saved shook his head and grabbed hold of me.

"Thank you for saving my life, Will," he said, smiling at me.

It was Akemi!

"Take your time," he said as I wheezed, trying to find my breath again.

"Will's had an idea," Zoe broke in. "He thinks he knows a way to get the ninjas off the mountain-top once and for all!"

They both looked at me expectantly. I pointed at my chest and did a lot of wheezing.

"Oh come on, Will!" said Zoe. "We haven't got time for you to do an impression of an asthmatic seal!"

Wheeze!

99

The battlefield looked even worse than when we had left it. There was no time to lose!

"Army of the Sun!" I cried, hovering high above the warriors. "Samurai friends! Fly upwards and take a sword!"

"No!" screamed the ninja leader.

He leaped towards me, but I was too high even for him to reach. He let out screeches of rage as samurai rose into the air all around him.

"It is good to have faith in others," said Shinobi as he took a dragon-scale sword from my hand. "You have not failed me, Will Solvit."

Bearing their new swords, the samurai flew back down to the ground. The ninjas were screaming with anger and frustration. As the samurai drew closer to them, the ninjas were jerked backwards. It looked as if an invisible hand was pulling them away.

"Retreat!" ordered their leader through gritted teeth. "There is nothing we can do!"

The ninjas poured back over the edge of the mountain and swarmed down to safety. Their leader watched them go, standing on the very brink of the mountain. Shinobi landed in front of him and the two men faced each other.

"This isn't over," said the ninja.

He pulled down his black mask. His face was twisted with hatred.

"Accept the way things are," said Shinobi, wearing a

One mean ninja...!!!

kind expression. "You can never take the Spring of Truth with hatred and greed in your heart."

But the Moon Dog leader did not want to hear what Shinobi had to say.

"We'll return here one day," he said, spitting out the words as if they were venom. "We'll come back and have our revenge on you all!"

Then he turned, scrambled over the edge of the mountain-top, and was gone.

I gazed around at the devastation of the battlefield. It was only a small area, but blood had been spilled and warriors had been slain. There would be a ton of clearing up to do.

Then I looked at the samurai who were still standing. They were so brave and so skilful. I never wanted them to have to go through anything like that again.

"Master Shinobi," I said, "these swords are

made with dragon scales. They will keep your enemies away from this place forever . . . if you'll trust me one last time."

Shinobi bowed to me and I turned to face the samurai.

"These swords need to be positioned all around the edge of the mountain-top," I said.

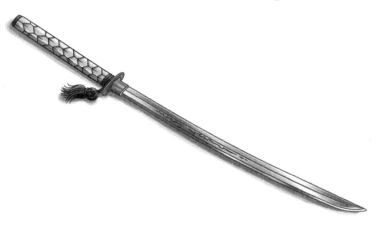

"Each of you, take your sword to the edge and drive it into the ground. Make sure they're all an equal distance apart."

The warriors did as I asked, and within a few minutes there was a gleaming protective barrier stretching all the way around the mountain-top. The Moon Dogs would never be able to come near them again!

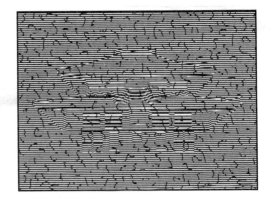

CHAPTER TEN
FAREWELLS

Once again, Zoe and I stood inside the secret heart of the temple, gazing at the bubbling spring and the engraved sword.

"The Spring of Truth is safe, thanks to you," said Shinobi. "I would like it to stay that way."

"The dragon-scale swords should keep all enemies away," I told him.

"I want to be sure that the future is safe for the spring," said Shinobi.

He picked up the engraved sword and laid it flat across his palms.

"This was made by the greatest sword-maker in all Japan," he said. "It is truly a work of art, as well as a labour of love."

The sword's inner glow was even more obvious now that I was so close to it. I placed my hand on the blade, very gently. It was warm to the touch.

"It's awesome," I said.

"It's dangerous," said Shinobi in a harder tone of voice. "It is written evidence of the spring's powers. Will, it cannot stay here any longer."

"But surely it belongs here?" I exclaimed.

"It is only a thing," said Shinobi. "It is an object, and objects do not matter. If the sword leaves this place, there will be no written clue to the spring's powers. One day their legend will be nothing more than a magical myth."

"Is that really what you want?" I asked.

"This is not about what I want," said Shinobi. "This is about what is best for the spring and how I can best keep my vow to protect it."

Finally I understood.

"How can I help?" I asked.

"I can see farewells in your faces," said the old man. "Take the sword with you when you go. Find a place to hide it where it can never be found by our enemies. Find a place where the wrong hands can never seize it."

A vision of Grandpa's attic sprang into my mind. The sword could join the many other secrets that lived in there.

"I know just the place," I said. "Don't worry; I promise it will be safe."

Zoe grinned at me – she knew exactly what I was thinking!

"What about you, Akemi?" she asked, turning to the boy-warrior. "Are you going to move on, now that you know the spring is safe?"

"The spring is only safe when loyal samurai are watching over it," Akemi replied. "There is nowhere I would rather be than on this mountain-top, riding the wind and watching over the Spring of Truth."

He bowed to us as three samurai warriors entered the room. Each of them was carrying something. They stood in front of us in a row and Shinobi gave a smile.

"We have some farewell presents for you both," he said. "First, the sheath for the engraved sword."

The first samurai stepped forward and handed me a leather sheath. I slipped the sword into it and put it into my rucksack next to my sword.

"Now, your samurai robes," said Shinobi. "You have passed our trials and you are now samurai of the Army of the Sun for all time."

The other two samurai stepped forwards with a robe each for Zoe and me, as well as armour and headdresses.

"Thank you!" we said.

I couldn't wait to try my new things on! They looked mega-cool. I wondered if I'd get away with wearing them at school . . .

"The third gift is not something you can see or touch," said Shinobi, "and yet it is the greatest gift of all. No matter where or when you travel, you will keep the ability to ride the wind. One sip from the Spring of Truth is enough for a lifetime."

Zoe looked delighted, shocked and amazed – all at the same time.

With one last rattle, Morph skidded to a stop.

"Woah," said Zoe, rubbing her head. "That was a rough ride."

"It never used to be that bad when Dad was in control," I said, swallowing hard. "I reckon Morph's on a bit of a power kick these days."

As if in response, Morph's door flew open with a bang. I laughed.

"Just kidding," I said, patting Morph's control panel. "Don't get your cables in a tangle."

Zoe picked up her samurai robe and stepped out.

"Are we back?" I asked.

"Yep," she replied. "Back in your room. It looks – and smells – just the same."

I followed her out with my robe and backpack, and Morph dwindled down to miniature size. Just then Grandpa Monty came into my room. ☺

Ha, yeah –
totally fresh...
NOT!!

"Did you find anything?" he asked.

"Huh?" I asked, trying to remember what we had been talking about before I left. "Oh yeah . . . your diary!"

"Ah," said Grandpa, producing a magnifying glass from his pocket and peering through it at me. "I know that look of confusion. You've already been and come back, haven't you?"

"Grandpa, it was awesome!" I began. "We went to –"

"Will?" said Zoe.

I turned to look at her. She was in classic Zoe pose – arms folded and foot tapping on the floor.

"Fancy a skateboard practice?" she asked.

She was eyeballing me in a way that told me it was an order, not a question.

"Sure," I said, grabbing my skateboard from the corner of my room.

Girls!!!

Luckily, Zoe had left her board here last time. She picked it up and raised her eyebrows at me.

"See you later, Grandpa!" I said.

"Indeed, Benjamin," he murmured.

He was now peering at my bedroom curtains through his magnifying glass. I left him to it and followed Zoe out into the garden.

CHAPTER ELEVEN
AN OMINOUS LETTER

"So what's with the look?" I asked as soon as we were in the garden and out of earshot.

"Well, for starters, you were about to start telling him all about the Adventure," said Zoe. "Have you forgotten your oath already?"

She was right! I had promised to say nothing about the Army of the Sun's secrets, and that meant telling no one about the Adventure – not even Grandpa.

"OK," I admitted. "I won't forget again."

"Plus, I can't wait to find out if we can still ride the wind," Zoe added. "No one can see us here."

Riding the wind ROCKS!

We sat on the topmost branch of the tree.

"OK," I said. "And let's promise never to ride the wind in front of anyone else either. I mean, if any grown-ups found out about it, they'd probably try to lock us up."

"Or do experiments on us," Zoe agreed. "OK, here goes." She put her hand over her heart. "I, Zoe, promise that I will never tell or show anyone anything about riding the wind. Now you say it."

I made the oath too, and then we shook hands.

"You want another ride?" she asked.

"I want dinner!" I said, suddenly realizing how hungry I was. "Let's go in – I've got a feeling Grandpa said something about making peppermint pancakes tonight."

We flew down from the tree and headed in for dinner. Just as we got to the front door, I realized that I had left my skateboard at the top of the

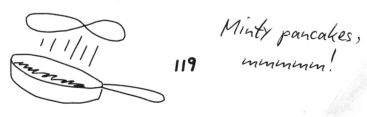

Minty pancakes, mmmmmm!

oak tree!

"I'd better go and get it before someone notices it and starts asking questions!" I said. "You go ahead, but don't eat all the pancakes!"

I sprinted back to the tree, took a quick look around to make sure that Stanley wasn't watching me, and then flew up to the top branch.

"No way!" I exclaimed.

There was my skateboard . . . with a white envelope taped to it!

"That was fast work!" I said, wondering for the millionth time who was leaving the letters for me.

My stomach was growling in hunger, but I couldn't wait to find out what the letter said. Hopefully it would give me a clue about my next Adventure! I ripped the envelope open and read it with a growing sense of horror.

WHAT KIND OF TREE CAN FIT INTO YOUR HAND?
A PALM TREE!

YOU DID A GREAT JOB IN ANCIENT JAPAN!

THANKS TO YOU, THE ARMY OF THE SUN IS ABLE TO KEEP THEIR SECRET SAFE.

IT'S BRILLIANT THAT YOU'RE HAVING FUN RIGHT NOW. YOU SHOULD MAKE THE MOST OF IT.

DO YOU KNOW HOW LUCKY YOU ARE TO HAVE A FRIEND LIKE ZOE?

YOU SHOULD TELL HER WHAT A GREAT FRIEND SHE IS BEFORE YOU MISS YOUR CHANCE.

PRETTY SOON, SHE'S GOING TO BE IN DEADLY DANGER.

P.S. DON'T FORGET TO HIDE THE SWORD.

A huge wave of fear rolled over me. I flew down to the ground with my skateboard tucked under my arm and walked back to the house, reading the letter 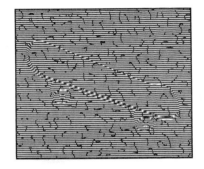 again. I guess I was hoping it might sound better the second time round, but it sounded worse.

I shoved the letter into my pocket as I walked into the house. There was no point in showing it to Zoe – it wasn't as if it gave her any kind of warning. I could hear her in the kitchen, chatting to Grandpa and playing with Plato. Suddenly I knew that I couldn't face Zoe straight away. I raced up the spiral staircase and into my room. The swords were still in my backpack. I took them out and carried them up to the attic.

There's something peaceful about the attic. I returned the original sword to its place on the wall, placed the engraved sword on an empty shelf and breathed in the warm, musty air.

It was weird – the attic was a world away from the sunlit mountain-top, and yet there was something about it that reminded me of being with Akemi, listening to his gentle voice.

Suddenly I felt a bit better. Whatever was going to happen in the future, moping around now wasn't going to help! Plus, the letter had given me some good advice. I left the attic and went down to the kitchen.

"Just in time," said Zoe, grinning at me. "Your grandpa's already started the second batch."

I slid into my seat and poured chocolate sauce over a peppermint pancake. For once, Grandpa had made something delicious.

"Thanks for coming with me on the Adventure this time," I said.

"No worries," said Zoe, stuffing half a pancake into her mouth.

"You see, you're my best friend," I said, abruptly.

Zoe looked at me in astonishment and stopped chewing.

"Er, thanks," she said. "Will, are you OK?"

I took a deep breath,

"I just wanted to tell you that I know I'm lucky to have a friend like you," I said.

Zoe frowned, folded her arms and narrowed her eyes.

"OK, Time Boy, what's going on?"

I couldn't help but laugh. Trust my best friend to make me see the funny side of trouble! I'd worry about danger when danger turned up, and until then . . .

"Pass me another pancake!" I said.

WILL SOLVIT AND THE KNIGHTS OF REVENGE

Barnaby came at me fast.

I ducked and pointed my lance at his chest.

OTHER BOOKS IN THE SERIES